Lola Fanola

First published in 2008

Text copyright © Penny Dolan 2008
Illustration copyright © Bruno Robert 2008

Wayland
338 Euston Road
London NW1 3BH

Wayland Australia
Level 17/207 Kent Street
Sydney, NSW 2000

Series Editor: Louise John
Editor: Katie Powell
Cover design: Paul Cherrill
Design: D.R.ink
Consultant: Shirley Bickler

A CIP catalogue record for this book is available from the British Library.

ISBN 9780750255363

Printed in China

Wayland is a division of Hachette Children's Books,
an Hachette Livre UK Company

www.hachettelivre.co.uk

Lola Fanola

Written by Penny Dolan
Illustrated by Bruno Robert

WAYLAND

Lola Fanola was the star of Carlo's Circus.

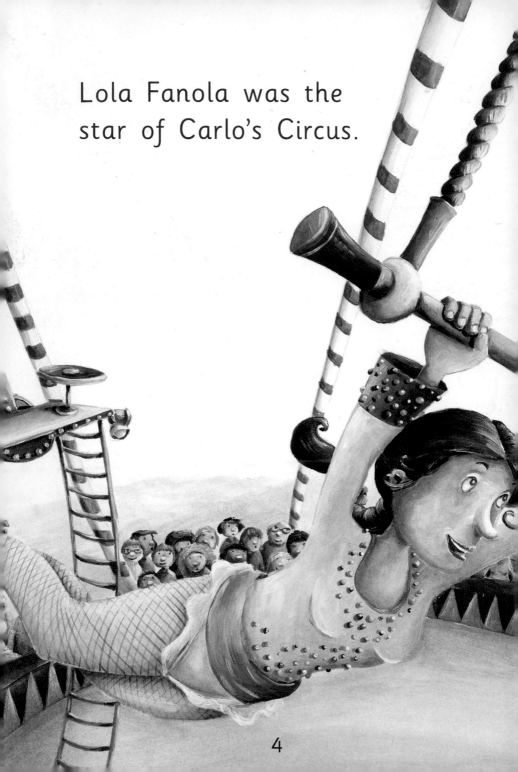

She swung on the
high trapeze.

5

But Lola made Jimmy swing on the low trapeze.

She made him walk on the
long, low beam.

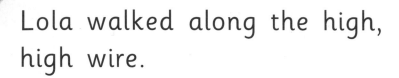

Lola walked along the high, high wire.

8

"Hooray for Lola Fanola!"
everyone cried.

"Let me swing on the high trapeze," said Jimmy. "Let me walk on the high wire. I can do it."

"No," said Lola. "I am the only star of the high trapeze!"

One day, just before their act,
Lola was hungry.

She ate a big, fat,
jammy doughnut!

As Lola danced and pranced on the high wire, a hungry wasp flew down.

It sat on the jam on Lola's nose.

"Help!" Lola cried.
She began to wobble.

Jimmy grabbed the high trapeze.

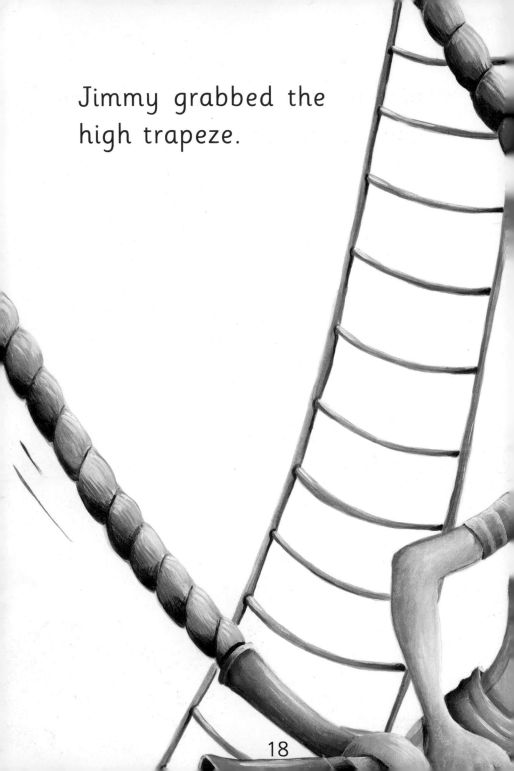

"Hold on, Lola!" he cried. "I'm coming to get you!"

Jimmy swung out on the trapeze, and he grabbed Lola as she fell.

"Oooh!" went the crowd.

"You saved me, Jimmy," said Lola. "You are the star of the circus show today!"

START READING is a series of highly enjoyable books for beginner readers. **The books have been carefully graded to match the Book Bands widely used in schools.** This enables readers to be sure they choose books that match their own reading ability.

Look out for the Band colour on the book in our Start Reading logo.

The Bands are:

Pink Band 1

Red Band 2

Yellow Band 3

Blue Band 4

Green Band 5

Orange Band 6

Turquoise Band 7

Purple Band 8

Gold Band 9

START READING books can be read independently or shared with an adult. They promote the enjoyment of reading through satisfying stories supported by fun illustrations.

Penny Dolan had great fun writing about Carlo's Circus, because she could pretend she was an expert juggler, brave trapeze artist, cheeky clown and an amazing elephant rider — even though she's definitely not!

Bruno Robert lives and works in Normandy, France, where he was born. He always wanted to draw and play with colours. When he is illustrating a story like this one, he likes to think of a bright and colourful world that is full of humour.